LEG TENDON
HEART VALVE
KIDNEY
EGG
BONE
T. TRUX
JAW
HEART PISTON
EYE
TAIL SECTION
NEURON
TOOTH
STOMACH
ELBOW
JOINT
?
P9-BZB-570

Millions of years ago, prehistoric trucks ruled

the earth! They were called DINOTRUX.

Millions of years later, their rusty

remains were found and put

into a great museum.

But the DINOTRUX

were growing

**For Andrea S.—the best of the best**

Copyright © 2012 by Chris Gall

All rights reserved. Except as permitted under the U.S. Copyright Act of 1976, no part of this publication may be reproduced, distributed, or transmitted in any form or by any means, or stored in a database or retrieval system, without the prior written permission of the publisher.

Little, Brown and Company

Hachette Book Group
237 Park Avenue, New York, NY 10017
Visit our website at www.lb-kids.com

Little, Brown and Company is a division of Hachette Book Group, Inc.
The Little, Brown name and logo are trademarks of Hachette Book Group, Inc.
The publisher is not responsible for websites (or their content) that are not owned by the publisher.

First Edition: May 2012

ISBN 978-0-316-13288-6

10 9 8 7 6 5 4 3 2

SC

Printed in China

The artwork in this book was created with the help of 30W synthetic motor oil, 4-bolt mains, and a competition clutch.
The text was set in Ritafurey, and the display type is BigNoodleTitling.

Many thanks to Miranda Stewart for suggesting the name *Velocitractor*.

IMMATURE MALE

REVENGE OF THE DINOTRUX
CHRIS GALL
LB
LITTLE, BROWN AND COMPANY
NEW YORK BOSTON
FOSSILIZED HEART

It wasn't fun being stuck in a drafty museum. The Dinotrux were poked, prodded, studied, and shaken. Their joints were so achy they couldn't move on their own.

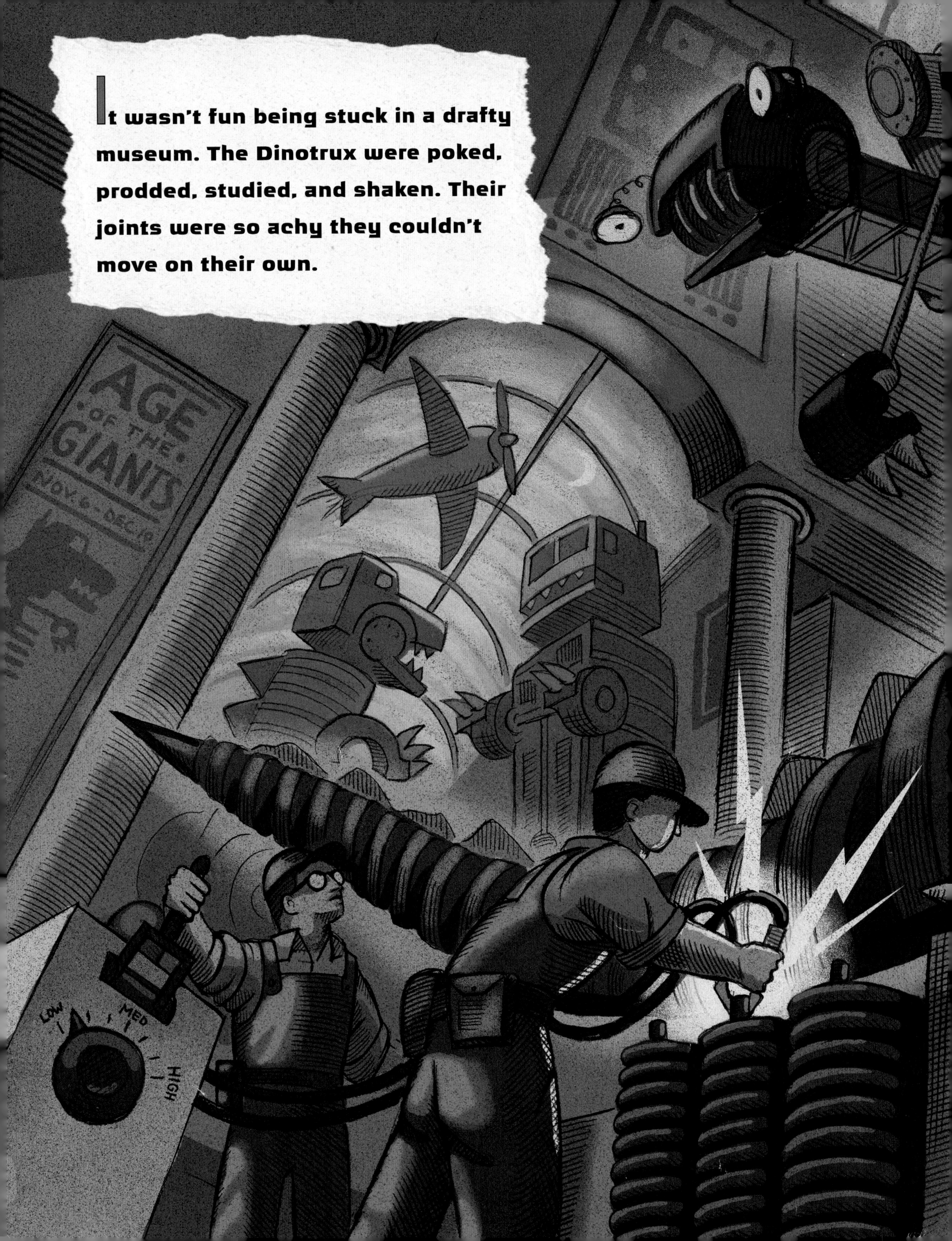

**Every day they needed their batteries recharged so that overexcited visitors could make the Dinotrux exhibits move.**

TYRANNOSAURUS TRUX was not happy. It was Kindergarten Day at the museum, and that meant lots of . . .

SCREAMING!

WHICH CAME FIRST?

BANGING!

SWINGING!

AND CHEWING GUM!

That night, TYRANNOSAURUS TRUX found sticky gum all over his claws and finally lost his temper. With a roar, he flicked the battery charger to HIGH and crashed through the museum wall. The rest of the supercharged Dinotrux rumbled right behind him.

HONNNKKKKKK!

"THE DINOTRUX WANT REVENGE!"
CLANKING.
GRINDING.

ROARInG!

A curious CRANEOSAURUS
peeked in windows.
NEWS
WHAT DO THEY WANT?

GARBAGEADON hadn't eaten in a million years. Boy, was he hungry!

Dastardly DUMPLODUCUS collected houses.

The VELOCITRACTORS did some landscaping on Main Street.

Sneaky **SEPTISAURUS**
gulped down a swimming pool.

SLUUUUUURP!

CEMENTOSAURUS left
a present in the town square.

And the angry roar of
TYRANNOSAURUS TRUX
could be heard all over the city.

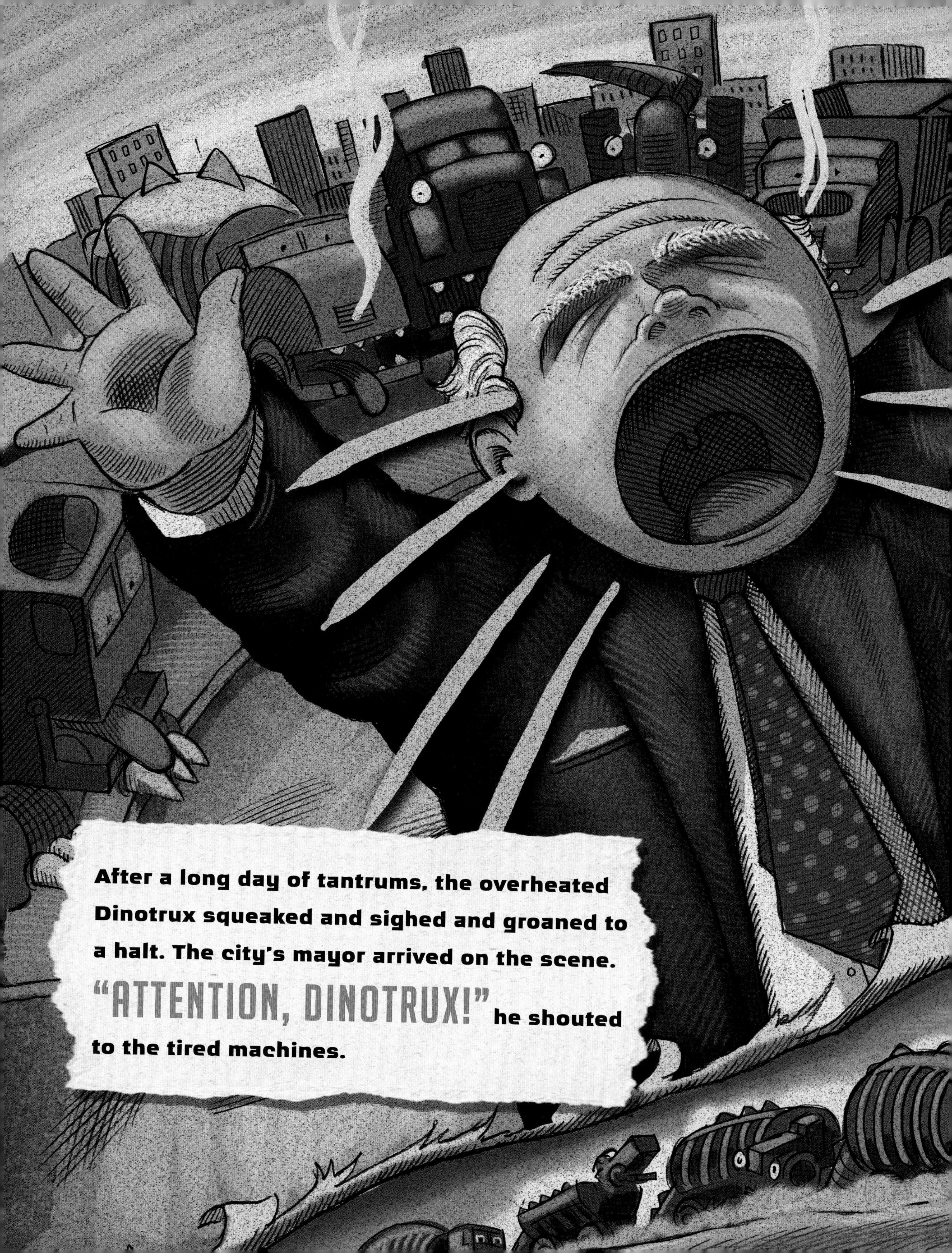

After a long day of tantrums, the overheated Dinotrux squeaked and sighed and groaned to a halt. The city's mayor arrived on the scene. **"ATTENTION, DINOTRUX!"** he shouted to the tired machines.

"This is not how modern trucks behave. You must go to school and learn new ways," he declared.

At first they behaved like typical Dinotrux. **SEMISAURUS** played with pencils.

**ROLLODON** rearranged the chairs.

**MINERDON** tried to escape.

**GARBAGEADON**
had a snack.

And **TYRANNOSAURUS TRUX**
was especially naughty!

But soon the Dinotrux learned to help.
The children taught them to read.

**And together they discovered some books they just couldn't put down.**

Then one day, the Dinotrux didn't come back from recess. Neither did the children. The anxious teachers found a giant hole in the fence.

"THE DINOTRUX ARE ON THE LOOSE AGAIN!"
ESCAPE FROM ALCATRAZ

A great search led them to the woods outside of town, where they heard a terrible commotion.

They were afraid to look! But when they peeked through the trees, they couldn't believe what they saw. . . .

**The Dinotrux had built a playground! And it was just perfect for . . .**

**SCREAMING!**

**BANGING!**

SWINGING!

THYROID
VOICE BOX
FINGER BONE
TOE
TOE
LUNG
SKIN SECTION
EGG CASE
SYNAPSE
CONTROL
EYE
T. TRUX TEETH
BIRTH OF YOUNG
CEREBRAL CORTEX